Tales from Acorn Wood

Three lift-the-flap stories

Julia Donaldson

Axel Scheffler

MACMILLAN CHILDREN'S BOOKS

First published 2006 by Macmillan Children's Books
This edition published 2008 by Macmillan Children's Books
Rabbit's Nap, Postman Bear and *Hide-and-Seek Pig* first published 2000
by Macmillan Children's Books
a division of Macmillan Publishers Limited
20 New Wharf Road, London N1 9RR
Basingstoke and Oxford
Associated companies throughout the world
www.panmacmillan.com

ISBN: 978-1-4050-9025-4

5 7 9 8 6 4

A CIP catalogue record for this book is available from the British Library.

Printed in Malaysia

Rabbit's Nap

Rabbit's feeling sleepy.
She curls up in a chair.

Tap! Tap! Who's that?
Oh dear! It's Builder Bear.

Where can Rabbit have her nap?
The window seat looks nice.

Bang! Clash! Who's that?
Oh no! A band of mice.

Rabbit's in her deckchair.
A doze would be so good.

Whack! Crack! Who's that?
It's Fox – he's chopping wood.

"A shady tree!" says Rabbit.
"The kind of spot I like."

Ting-a-ling! Who's that?
It's Tortoise on his bike.

Poor tired Rabbit goes back home.
She yawns and rubs her eyes.

Rat-a-tat! Who's that?
"Your friends with a surprise!"

"Hush-a-bunny! Tra-la-la!
We'll sing you off to sleep!"

Zzzzz! Zzzzz! What's that?
Shall we have a peep?

Postman Bear

Bear is writing letters.
One, two, three.

Bear goes out to post them.
Who lives in this tree?

Shall we count the letters?

Only two.

Someone's home is in this pond.
Let's find out who.

Just one letter left now.
Who's it for?

Someone's made a heap of earth.

Who's behind this door?

What was in those letters,
One, two, three?

Would you like to open one?

Have a look and see.

Bear is in the kitchen.
Watch him cook.

What's inside the oven?

Let's have a look.

Someone's knocking at the door.
One, two, three.

Bear goes to open it.
Who can it be?

"Happy Birthday, Bear!"

Hide-and-Seek Pig

"Let's play hide and seek," says Hen.
"Yes," says Pig. "I'll count to ten."

Now it's time for Pig to seek.
Can you see a yellow beak?

"Come on, Blackbird, follow me.
Let's find Hen. Where can she be?"

Look! A tent! Is Hen in here?
Can you see a long brown ear?

"Come on, Rabbit, follow me.
Let's find Hen. Where can she be?"

Pig has found a spotty sheet.
Can you see a pair of feet?

"Come on, Squirrel, follow me.
Let's find Hen. Where can she be?"

Maybe Hen's behind this pail.
Can you see a furry tail?

"Come on, Dormouse, follow me.
Let's find Hen. Where can she be?"

Who's behind this garden rose?
Can you see a stripy nose?

"Come on, Badger, follow me.
I'll lead you to our picnic tea."

Still no Hen! Where did she go?
Pig can't think. But do you know?